Ragged Island Mysteries™

No Laughing Matter

by Rosie Bensen

Mc Graw Hill **Wright Group**
McGraw-Hill

To my four Ragged friends, with love and plenty of laughing matter

No Laughing Matter
Text copyright © Rosie Bensen
Illustrations copyright © Wright Group/McGraw-Hill
Illustrations by Taylor Bruce

Ragged Island Mysteries™ is a trademark of The McGraw-Hill
Companies, Inc.

Wright Group/McGraw-Hill
19201 120th Avenue NE, Suite 100
Bothell, WA 98011
www.WrightGroup.com

Printed in the United States of America

10 9 8 7 6 5 4 3

ISBN: 0-322-01587-1
ISBN: 0-322-01653-3 (6-pack)

TABLE OF CONTENTS

Chapter		Page

Table of Contents

1

TWO LEFT FEET

"YOU'RE PULLING MY BRAINS OUT, Marla!" twelve-year-old Liz French yelled as her older sister tried to yank a comb through her brown curls.

"Combs are better for your hair than brushes," Marla said. And she should know. After all, she was The Beautiful Marla and a junior in high school. She was a regular fashion encyclopedia. Liz knew Marla always combed her honey-colored hair. She also knew that the shade of honey changed quite often.

The sisters were sitting on Liz's bed. They shared a bedroom. At least that was the idea. Marla's beauty products and clothes took up most of it. Liz caught sight of her face in the mirror. She clamped her mouth shut over her crooked teeth. Soon they'd be covered with braces. She'd look even goofier.

"Liz, look at your nails! Chewed to the quick—again," Marla said.

"At least you won't have to waste any blue glitter nail polish on them," Liz said, rubbing her sore scalp.

Their orange cat, Bones, hopped onto Liz's lap.

"Why don't you go to this dumb dance for me, Bones," Liz said. "You're a much better dancer than I'll ever be. The boys will line up on one side of the gym and the girls on the other. We'll all feel like we're lining up for a parade."

Marla opened a jar of blue eye shadow. She set it down on the table and dabbed one finger into it.

"Don't you dare!" Liz shouted. She jumped up, sending Bones leaping toward the mirror. On his way, he got one front paw stuck in the eye shadow jar. He shook the paw until the jar flew off onto the floor. The mirror fell forward and cracked. "I really don't need this. Seven years of bad luck. I feel sick."

"You're just nervous. You'll relax when you start dancing," Marla said.

"As if I'm going to dance," Liz said. She sneezed. "See, Marla? I'm allergic to all this goop." She was allergic to dust and ragweed. Why not makeup?

"LISTEN TO ME, LOU..." Liz's mother's voice echoed down the hall of the Rocky Point Bed and Breakfast. Good thing there were no guests tonight.

Liz froze. Marla wiped up blue paw prints from the table.

"They even fight with miles of water between them," Liz groaned.

4

Liz and Marla's mother, Jean, had stayed on Ragged Island after the divorce. Lou, their father, now had an apartment on the mainland in Bellport. Liz and Marla spent weekends there. Their father sold real estate.

"Marla, why can't they talk to each other without fighting?" Liz asked.

Marla screwed on the lid of the eye shadow. "Chemistry. They're stuck with the wrong chemistry."

"But it's not fair to stick us with it too," Liz sighed. Her stomach felt worse.

"You have to get used to it," Marla said. "It's our only choice." She stood back to look at Liz. "Just a little eye shadow..."

"NO WAY!"

"Mrs. Davies is here, Liz," Jean French called from downstairs.

Liz raced away from her sister and out into the crisp fall night. Allie Davies slid open the van door, and Liz jumped into the third row of seats. She wedged herself between Allie and her younger brother Daniel. The other Davies children, Ramon, Sasha, and Tomas, wriggled and giggled in the middle row.

"Hi, Liz," Mrs. Davies said. "All dolled up for the dance?"

"Impossible," Liz said. She shrank deeper into the seat.

Allie elbowed her in the side. They both laughed. Liz tried to run her fingers through her hair. They got stuck. She had to pull them out. Allie's black hair was so straight and smooth it hardly ever needed combing or brushing.

"Remind me why we're doing this," Liz said to her friend.

"Because we promised Jinx," Allie said.

Jinx Harris, Liz's cousin, had been one of

the organizers of the dance.

"I wouldn't do this for anyone else," Liz said.

"Not even Drew?" Allie said with a grin.

Liz liked her classmate Drew Ellis. In fact, she liked him a lot.

"Okay. For Drew. Or you. But that's it," Liz said, crossing her arms fiercely. She noticed the backpack between Allie's feet. "You didn't bring your camera did you?"

Allie was serious about photography. She was the editor and chief photographer of the school paper. Liz helped her sometimes.

"Of course I did. A dance is hot news," Allie said.

"This is going from bad to worse," Liz moaned.

The decorations committee, headed by Lauren McBride, had chosen a 1960s neon colors theme. Liz took one dizzy look at the clashing stripes in the school gym. She thought she was going to throw up.

She closed her eyes for a moment. She opened them on Jinx, or rather on the top of Jinx's head. He was short for his age. But he more than made up for it in energy.

"How about these decorations. Aren't they gr-o-o-vy?" Jinx asked in a perfect imitation of a sixties hippie.

"You're even talking like you're from the '60s, Jinx," Allie said. She glanced around the gym. "No one's dancing. They have to dance so I can take pictures."

"If they see your camera, no one WILL dance," Liz complained.

"Lauren will," Allie said. "Won't she, Jinx? Go ask her."

"She'll probably say no," Jinx said. Lauren McBride was head cheerleader. She was cute, popular, and perfect. Jinx had a big crush on her.

The song ended. Mr. Blake, their sixth-grade teacher, spoke over the loudspeaker. "Next dance, everyone gets out there or I'll call off the soda bottle music project!"

A chorus of groaning echoed around the room. Everyone in sixth grade was looking forward to being in the soda bottle concert band. They had already made bananas into mummies earlier in the fall. Mr. Blake really knew how to make science fun.

So everyone in sixth grade found a partner. Liz searched for Drew. He was the tallest member of their class, so she spotted him easily. He must have read her mind. He was on his way over to her. Jinx was sidling up to Lauren. Allie headed for Steve McDonald, who drew cartoons for the newspaper.

The music started. Liz and Drew danced.

Or rather, they moved around. The wild rock number was torture. Drew winced. Liz knew he hated loud noise.

Liz watched Lauren. She danced just like a professional. Lauren's hair was shaped in a '60s style to match the theme of the dance. Her makeup was perfect. Her clothes were expensive and so '60s. Wouldn't Marla love to have her for a sister?

Liz felt like she had two left feet. The fact that she tripped Drew with one of them proved it. She reached to help him up.

"Sorry, Drew."

He laughed. "Let's get away from the speakers and grab some refreshments before Jinx eats them all."

They headed for the long table under the basketball scoreboard. Liz took a handful of popcorn even though she wasn't hungry.

"Here's a new couple."

They turned to see Mrs. Spawn, the school secretary, who was known behind her back as the Sergeant Major. "Are you two having a nice time?" Mrs. Spawn asked. She made it sound like dancing together meant you were going to get married. She smiled.

Liz wished she wouldn't. Her teeth were almost as brown as the coffee she constantly drank. She had dragon breath to match. Her greasy hair was pulled back into a tiny knot stuck with pins.

"By the way, Liz, I need to get your father's new phone number. I realized the other day I only have your mother's number."

Liz felt her face get hot. Only yesterday, in the middle of a crowded school office, Mrs. Spawn had asked her, "Now where shall I send this notice, Bellport or Rocky Point?"

Didn't the school just send things to both addresses when parents got divorced?

"Well, just let me know," Mrs. Spawn shouted over the music. "I need to keep my records straight. These parents do make it a challenge."

Divorce was bad enough without Mrs. Spawn making such a huge deal about it. Liz took a step back from the coffee fumes.

Mrs. Spawn turned to look at the dance floor. "Just look at that Lauren. She was born to dance."

Drew whispered, "And born to be every teacher's pet. Let's get some punch."

When they were a safe distance away, Liz turned to Drew. "What a witch. No wonder her husband didn't come to the dance with her. I'm so sick of that woman. I could scream!"

"You COULD scream in this place, and nobody would hear," Drew said.

"I HATE HER!" Liz yelled. Then she clamped her hand over her mouth.

Drew laughed and pointed. Mrs. Spawn had not heard. She was twisting, by herself, to a dumb '60s song, "The Joker."

2
RAGGED FOUR

"We're shorthanded for today's game," Mr. Blake said.

Liz, Jinx, and Drew stood with their soccer teammates in a circle around their teacher and coach. Liz was the only girl on the team. Jinx's big mutt, Chief, sat in the middle of the circle. Liz spotted Allie with her camera on the sidelines. Allie was also sports editor for the newspaper.

"Maybe Lauren would play," Jinx said.

"Oh, right," Liz said. "And give up her

chance to do her pom-pom thing? No way."

"I guess you're right," Jinx said.

"And Allie's busy taking pictures," Drew added.

Chief suddenly saw a squirrel and tore across the soccer field. He knocked Jinx over on his way out of the circle.

Mr. Blake laughed. "Where's that extra jersey? We'll suit Chief up." Mr. Blake loved a good joke.

During warm-ups, he approached Liz. "I heard there's going to be a regional cross-country meet next week, Liz. You're our fastest runner. I know you work out regularly. You interested?"

"Yes," she said.

Liz loved to run. It was one thing she knew she was good at.

Chief streaked past them, chasing a stray

ball. He was wearing a soccer shirt with the number 00.

"How did you hold him still long enough to get that on him?" Liz asked, laughing.

Mr. Blake laughed too. "Drew did it."

Liz smiled. Drew was strong, and he was used to animals. His mother was a veterinarian. He sometimes helped with her animals.

"Maybe I'll sign Chief up for the cross-country meet too," Mr. Blake said.

"He runs with me sometimes when he isn't chasing Bones," Liz said.

"Who's Bones?" Mr. Blake asked.

"Our cat." Liz looked beyond Mr. Blake. She could see Lauren's brother, Owen, kicking a ball with Daniel Davies on the sidelines. They were both in third grade. The ball kept hitting Owen in the face and knocking his thick, wire-rimmed glasses off.

"Poor Owen," Drew said, joining Liz after Mr. Blake left. "He can't see very well even with those glasses on. They seem to fall off at the drop of a—"

"Soccer ball," Liz laughed. Her laughter died quickly. "Oh, no. Ma AND Pop are here." And they were already arguing about something. Liz could tell by the rigid set of her mother's face. Her father kept running his hand over his thinning hair. No wonder it was falling out.

"I TOLD YOU I NEEDED THE MONEY FOR REPAIRS ON THE PLUMBING," Ma said, too loudly.

"I DON'T HAVE IT RIGHT NOW," Pop said. "I CAN'T VERY WELL PAY IT IF I DON'T HAVE IT, CAN I?"

Liz couldn't believe her parents were fighting here, in front of the whole school. Her father looked up at a passing cloud. Maybe he thought some money would drop out of it and solve all his problems.

Liz felt butterflies declare war on each other in her stomach. She never used to feel this way. Was it because of the game? Or was it because her parents couldn't get along anywhere? To make matters worse, she saw Mrs. Spawn arrive and take up a position too close to her parents. Liz wanted

to run over and throw a bag over Mrs. Spawn's ugly head.

She looked away. On the opposite side of the field Lauren and two other cheerleaders jumped and flipped.

Liz rubbed her stomach.

"You okay?" Allie asked as she loaded new film into her camera.

"I just wish Ma and Pop wouldn't come to stuff together."

"Even if they didn't fight?" Allie asked.

"And when is THAT ever going to happen?" Liz asked.

Allie could only shake her head. "Look, at least they're moving away from each other."

Liz looked. She breathed a sigh of relief. But she again noticed Mrs. Spawn.

"My second wish is that the field would open up and swallow Mrs. Spawn," Liz whispered.

"That's fine by me. I won't miss her," Allie said. "Third wish? You get three."

Liz thought for a moment. "Let's meet with Jinx and Drew after the game. I'll tell you my third wish then. And THAT wish will come true."

The Ragged Island team lost the game. They were used to losing this year. Afterward, Liz, Drew, Jinx, and Allie biked to First Beach on the south side of the island.

They leaned their bikes against the tall pines near the sand. They walked down to the shore and decided to build a castle. Allie organized their efforts. Drew dug deep holes. Jinx jumped in and out of them like a kangaroo. Liz dripped decorations of wet sand on the turrets and towers.

"Okay, Liz. Third wish time," Allie said.

"I'm sick of Mrs. Spawn," Liz began.

"What else is new?" Jinx asked.

"No, I mean REALLY sick. Every chance she gets she makes some comment about my parents."

"Like, 'Where should I send this report card?'" Jinx perfectly imitated the school secretary.

"Exactly," Liz said.

"I hate the way she tries to get me a detention every time I get to school late," Drew said. His father owned and ran Mel's

Diner. He had injured his back working as a stone mason years ago. Some mornings he could hardly get out of bed. On those days Drew opened the diner and arrived at school late.

"Sergeant Major Spawn won't let up on me about—" Jinx began angrily.

"Lauren," Allie finished for him. "Mrs. Spawn minds everyone's business. She won't let me forget about getting the captions mixed up in the newspaper."

"Big deal. So you labeled the principal as the animal control officer," Drew said.

"He IS one, if you think about it," Jinx said.

"You should label her School Witch," Liz said, frowning. "So we all agree she's a huge pain?"

The others nodded.

"Then I say we pull some pranks on her."

"Pranks..." Allie muttered.

Liz could see she was already designing one.

"Cool!" Jinx said. "We can call ourselves the Ragged Four."

Drew nodded.

"Each of us plans one prank," Liz said.

"No one quits until they're all done," Allie said. "And no one tells."

They placed their hands together for a group shake.

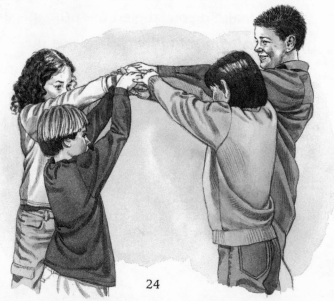

"I've already got mine," Jinx said. "I'll do a crank call."

"Perfect," Liz said. "But it has to be nasty."

"Wait a minute," Drew said. "I thought you meant pranks. Jokes. Ha, ha. Funny. Like April Fool's Day."

"She's so MEAN, Drew. She doesn't deserve funny. She deserves nasty," Liz said.

"If it's a good prank, it'll be irritating enough," Jinx said.

"And we'll get to have all the laughs," Allie added.

Liz didn't agree. Nothing about Mrs. Spawn seemed funny to her. But she didn't say anything.

"I'll rig her chair so she can't turn it to get a view of everyone's business," Allie said. "I hate the way she spins around every time I go into the office."

25

"Okay," Liz said. "You can put tacks in the seat while you're at it."

"Funny, Liz. Remember?" Jinx said. "Not painful."

"You guys are such chickens," Liz said angrily.

Drew took his time. He dug up another armload of sand. Then he said, "Speaking of chickens, I could borrow an animal from the shelter. A kitten, maybe." He paused.

Everyone waited. Drew's mother, who worked at a clinic in Bellport, also ran an animal shelter at home.

"I could hide it in her desk drawer," he offered.

"Yes!" Liz said, beginning to smile. She had visions of cat poop lining the tidy drawers of Mrs. Spawn's desk.

"Would it be safe in there?" Allie asked. It was just like Allie to think of every possible detail.

"Bones hides in my clothes all the time," Liz said. "He likes my sweater drawer best."

"The desk drawer is nice and deep," said Drew. I'll be sure to leave it open a crack. And I'll make a miniature litter box for it too."

"I guess that's okay then," Allie said. "What's your prank, Liz?"

Liz dripped her tallest sand decoration on the highest tower of their castle. She watched the first wave erode the outside walls. She got up and brushed sand off her jeans.

"Mine will have to do with toothpaste, mouthwash, and gross breath," she said.

The others laughed so loud that they almost didn't hear the crash in the woods behind them.

"What was that?" Jinx asked.

"Must have been one of the bikes falling over," Allie said.

But when they walked back to get their bicycles, all four stood just as they had left them.

3
AND THE WINNER IS...

"Are you sure she's at her desk?" Jinx asked Liz.

After school the next day, they huddled together by the pay phone on the wall outside the school. Liz was holding her jacket around Chief. It was hard to keep the jacket over his wagging tail. Jinx held Chief's favorite squeak toy, Cozy Rooster, just out of reach.

"I checked," she said.

"Okay, here goes," Jinx said, calling the

school. He held the receiver so Liz could hear.

"Ragged Island School, Mrs. Spawn speaking."

Jinx disguised his voice. "Mrs. Spawn, my name is Bob Kirby of Prizes Unlimited. How would you like to be a winner?"

"We don't take these calls at school," she said. She hung up.

"What do I do now?" Jinx asked.

"Call again," Liz said. "Tell her that her name was chosen from the list of the one hundred best school secretaries in the country."

Jinx dialed again. Before Mrs. Spawn could say anything, he quickly told her how she had been selected. She took the bait.

"How do I know this is a real offer?" Mrs. Spawn asked.

"Madam, you will know when your prize

arrives! All you have to do is bark three times. If you make our prize dog, Stanley, answer your bark, YOU WIN!"

There was a pause.

"Don't hang up," Liz whispered.

"And, Mrs. Spawn," Jinx continued. "if you succeed in making Stanley squeak his dog toy, YOU GET A BONUS!"

Another pause. Then Mrs. Spawn let out three deafening barks. Liz giggled. Chief went wild. He jumped at the telephone and barked. He jumped at Jinx, grabbed the toy and squeaked it furiously.

"Congratulations, Mrs. Spawn," Jinx shouted. "YOU ARE A WINNER."

"What's my prize?

How about the bonus? When and where do I get them?" Mrs. Spawn asked.

Jinx looked at Liz. She mouthed the words "BOOBY PRIZE." Jinx shook his head.

"Your prize will be delivered to you right at school. Soon. It's a month's supply of kitty litter!"

"And the bonus? But, wait, Mr. Kirby. I don't have a cat!"

Jinx hung up. "Let's get out of here!"

He grabbed Chief's toy, and they ran to the playground, laughing. Chief trotted happily beside them. They avoided the office side of the building.

"Slow down. We don't want to look guilty," Liz said.

"Good work, Chief," Jinx said, patting the dog's head. "Now go home."

Chief rolled over.

"I said GO HOME!" Jinx shouted again.

Chief played dead. Liz burst out laughing. She laughed until her belly ached.

"We have to get rid of him. He's evidence," Jinx said.

Liz shouted, "GO GET BONES!"

Chief took off in the general direction of the Rocky Point Bed and Breakfast. Jinx stuffed the toy rooster in his jacket pocket.

They then saw a round, bald man climb out of a van. *Acme Kitchen Supplies* was printed in bright orange on the side panel.

"That's Mr. Spawn, isn't it?" Jinx asked.

"Yes. Poor guy," Liz said. Before she turned away, she saw that Mr. Spawn was stumbling under the weight of a large box. "He must be the most bossed-around husband in the universe."

"Living with Mrs. Spawn must be awful. Good thing he has to travel in his job," Jinx agreed. "At least he gets a break."

"We better go to soccer practice," Liz said.

They headed toward the gym to change. Liz threw down her backpack outside the door to the girls' locker room and leaned to get a drink from the fountain.

"Hey, are you trying to add salt to the gym floor?" Jinx laughed. He reached to pick up the salt carton that had slipped out of Liz's backpack.

"I'm bringing that home to Ma. I borrowed it for the banana project. It worked pretty well, sort of like salt cod, only this was salt banana. I put it in an old velvet jewelry box Ma had."

"Velvet? She let you use that for mummifying a banana?" Jinx asked.

"It was left over from something Pop gave her," Liz said. "She doesn't want to save any of that stuff now that they're divorced. She told me she hoped the banana would ruin the box."

"Did it?" Jinx asked.

"Sure did," Liz said. "And the banana turned into green mold. Just like their marriage."

4
AND THE LOSER IS...

"I just want to peek and see what she's doing," Liz said to Drew and Jinx after practice. "I wish Allie didn't have to babysit. She should see this too."

"You don't think Mrs. Spawn is actually waiting for her prize, do you?" Drew asked.

"It won't hurt to check," Jinx said.

"What if she sees us?" Drew asked.

"We'll just pretend we had to go back to homeroom for something," Liz said.

They slowed their pace as they passed the

door to the office. Owen McBride was standing in front of Mrs. Spawn's desk. She handed him a pile of papers.

"Thank you, Owen. Just take those to Mrs. Wilson's room. Then go find Lauren. She should be finished cheerleading by now," she said.

"I'd like to go find Lauren too," Jinx muttered.

"Easy, Jinx," Drew whispered.

Owen set the pile of papers down and straightened it. He picked it up again.

Mrs. Spawn smiled at him and took a sip from her ever-present mug.

Coffee exploded from Mrs. Spawn's mouth. It made Liz think of Mount Vesuvius, an erupting volcano. Coffee splattered freckles down the front of her purple suit. Coffee splattered the papers on her desk. Coffee even splattered Owen's glasses.

"Salt!" Mrs. Spawn sputtered. "My best suit is ruined! And look at this rug. And my papers." She looked around frantically. "I need a towel. I need help, and I need it immediately!"

Drew pulled Jinx and Liz away. "Come on, before she sees us," he said. "We don't want to be caught anywhere near here." They regrouped on the playground.

"What's the deal?" Jinx said, catching his breath. "I thought WE were the Ragged Four prank team. Someone is trying to get in on the action."

"Copycats," Drew agreed.

"But what a great idea," Liz said. "That really got her. Did you see what it did to that ugly suit? I bet it was Mr. Spawn. Remember we saw him going into school just before soccer. He was carrying a box. There could have been plenty of salt in there. He's probably been planning to put salt in her coffee for years."

"Quite the coincidence," Jinx said.

"What do you mean?" Liz asked.

"I mean that right after I do my prank, someone else does one," he said.

"Do you think we're the only people who want to get back at that woman? Get real, Jinx." Liz said.

"You've got a point," Drew said.

"Let's track down Mr. Spawn and see if he was delivering salt," Liz said.

"Good idea," Jinx said.

They searched the school. Each carried a book so it would look like they were on their way to study something.

"Hey. What's happening?" Liz recognized the nagging, nasal voice of Walter Pescatelli, sixth-grade clown, weak soccer goalie, and junk-food junkie.

Liz had to think quickly. "We're on our way to the kitchen to see if we can get a snack." She immediately realized this was a bad idea.

"Food? I'm with you," Walter said, falling in step beside them. He reached over his belly into one of his pockets and pulled out a handful of small packages: sugar, salt, pepper, ketchup, mustard. "I like to be

41

prepared for any kind of snack."

Drew gave him a long look. "Did you take those from my dad's diner?"

"I collect these whenever I make a fast food stop, Drewster," Walter said. "You never know when a good batch of fries will come along."

"You have salt?" Liz asked.

"Sure," Walter said. He showed her several packets to prove it.

They found Mr. Spawn in the kitchen. He was holding a metal strip.

"This attachment should clear up that problem you've been having with the slicer, Betty," he said.

The school cook, Mrs. Miller, nodded. "Drew, Walter, Jinx, and Liz," she said. "What brings you to my kitchen?"

"Snack hunt," Walter said.

"There are some cookies left from lunch

over on that counter," she said, smiling. "Help yourselves."

Liz approached the counter by way of Mr. Spawn's box, which was open on the floor. She peeked in and saw three boxes of salt. Everyone thanked Mrs. Miller and left the kitchen.

"I'll see you guys around," Walter said, through the cookie he had stuffed in his mouth.

"If only Mrs. Spawn had a personality like Mrs. Miller's," Jinx said after Walter had gone.

"For sure," Drew said.

"He had salt," Liz said.

"We know Walter had salt," Jinx said.

"No, I mean Mr. Spawn," Liz said. "I saw it in the box he delivered."

"So, do you think Mr. Spawn's our man?" Jinx asked.

Liz shook her head. "I don't know. I can see Walter doing it."

"It's his kind of thing," Drew agreed. He rubbed his brushy hair. "This is getting complicated."

"How about we cruise by the office one more time to check out the damage?" Liz asked. "We might find some other clues."

"No way," Drew said. "You don't want Mrs. Spawn to suspect us, do you? Give it a rest, Liz."

"What's to suspect?" Liz asked.

Jinx hesitated. "I'd better get home."

"Me too," Drew said.

"Cowards," Liz said to their backs. She walked to the office alone. When she got there, she found Lauren and Owen helping Mrs. Spawn clean up.

"I can't imagine who would do such a thing," Mrs. Spawn was saying. "I don't

know why all students can't be just like you,
Lauren, dear."

Liz saw Lauren frown as if she had just
taken a sip from Mrs. Spawn's mug. She
pushed back her glossy brown hair.

"Maybe somebody thought it was April,"
Owen said as he wiped coffee off Mrs.
Spawn's chair.

"April?" Lauren asked.

"April Fool's Day," Owen said. "Or maybe
he got excited and couldn't wait."

"April Fool's is foolish enough without
having it all year long," Mrs. Spawn
grumbled. "This suit..."

"Maybe the cleaners can fix it," Lauren
suggested.

Mrs. Spawn saw Liz. "Don't stand there
staring. Give us some help. We still haven't
wiped off all of these papers."

Liz winced at Mrs. Spawn's tone. She

quickly picked up some paper towels and rubbed at a spot on the desk. She caught Mrs. Spawn staring at her and rubbed harder. As she rubbed, she noticed fine white grains all over the desk. Salt. Whoever pulled this prank was either in a big hurry or didn't aim very well.

After a few more minutes Mrs. Spawn said, "Okay, children. I suppose that's about all we can do for now. Thank you, Lauren and Owen. Liz, you missed the worst of it."

When Liz got home, her mother asked her to mix a batch of scones for breakfast.

"The woman from New York wants to sleep late. I'll serve her breakfast if you'll just set the table, Liz," Ma said.

Liz thought, "And Marla gets out of doing anything—again." Marla went to school in Bellport and spent more time staying with Pop now.

Liz finished her chores. Then she went out for a run. She whistled for Chief as she neared Jinx's house. The dog loped easily beside her.

"You'd win that meet for sure, Chief," she told him. "That is, if you didn't get mixed up and play dead in the middle of it."

Chief stopped and sat down. Liz laughed and called him. They ran on together. Liz thought about how much she loved to run. She was really looking forward to the cross-country meet. When she was running the course, she wouldn't have to watch her parents fighting the way she had to at the soccer game. Suddenly she got a sharp stitch in her side. She had to walk the rest of the way home.

After dinner that night, Liz called Allie.

"Did you hear about the coffee?" Liz asked.

"Yes. Jinx called," Allie said. "I wish I could have seen it, although there were more than enough thrills and spills right here."

"It was the best. She spit coffee all over that sick green suit she wears just about every day," Liz laughed.

"Jinx said you tried to figure out who did. it, but there are too many suspects," Allie said.

"Just one too many," Liz said. "It's either Mr. Spawn or Walter the Pack Rat."

"So it's Drew's turn tomorrow?" Allie asked.

"Yes," Liz said. "I told him I'd meet him at the shelter in the morning."

"He's going to use a kitten? How about a black one?" Allie asked.

"For bad luck. Good idea," Liz agreed.

5

GEORGE GOES TO SCHOOL

Liz turned into Drew's driveway on her bike at seven the next morning. Drew stood at the side of his house near the door to the animal shelter.

"Dad's long gone. Mom just left for the Bellport clinic," he said. "Hurry."

Liz followed him into the shelter. A round of barking, mewing, and squeaking greeted them.

Liz saw several large white rats in one of the cages on the counter.

"Let's use a rat instead," she said, moving toward the cage.

Drew stopped short. "Are you nuts? A rat would bite her for sure."

"So? She deserves it."

Drew looked at Liz. He shook his head. "You're really mad at her."

Liz frowned. "Aren't you? She got Mr. Thornton to give you a detention last time you were late."

"I don't like her, you're right. But I don't hate her enough to wish a rat bite on her."

Liz did. But she looked at Drew and said, "Rats!"

He smiled. "That's more like it."

They went over to the kitten corner. A screen door held in a gang of at least fifteen. Liz spotted a black one behind the others. Several were clawing their way up the screen. They tried to cuff at Drew's hands as

50

he unlatched it.

"Allie suggested a black one," she said.

"We'll take George," Drew said. He reached for the tiny, dark fur ball.

George mewed. He blinked huge green eyes. He purred.

"George is pretty laid back," Drew said. "He won't mind spending an hour or two in a drawer. We'll put a piece of blanket in with him. And I have a small box of litter, too."

They tucked George into Drew's backpack.

"I'll close the door and catch up with you," Liz offered.

"Thanks. Be sure you shut it tight. Check the latch too," Drew said.

Liz pedaled fast and caught up with him as he turned onto Maine Street.

"Is George okay?" Liz called. She shivered as the fall breeze cut through her sweater. Ma had been right to suggest a jacket.

"He hasn't moved," Drew said. "Our biggest problem will be his purring."

When they reached school, they made their way to the office. Drew stopped now and then to listen for footsteps. Liz jogged ahead to peer through the doorway.

"Hurry, her coat's here," she whispered. "She's gone for coffee."

Drew slipped George out of his backpack and into the top drawer of Mrs. Spawn's desk. He set in the litter box and wrapped

the soft blanket scrap around the kitten. George's green eyes looked even bigger. "Good guy," Drew said, stroking the fuzzy head. He gently closed the drawer, leaving a small crack for air.

Liz heard footsteps. "The Sergeant Major's coming!"

"What'll we do?" Drew asked.

"Hide in the principal's office," Liz whispered.

"No way," Drew said.

Liz knew he hated that office. But they had no choice. Mrs. Spawn's high heels clicked closer and closer. Liz and Drew tiptoed into Mr. Thornton's office.

They hid behind his desk.

"I don't want to be in here," Drew whispered. "It was bad enough last week."

Liz looked around. "Lucky we're on the first floor. We'll climb out the window."

Opening that window sounded like a train rumbling through. They scrambled out. Drew pulled it shut.

"She's coming in!" he said, ducking.

They flattened themselves against the wall. Liz felt a sneeze coming. She looked down. She'd landed on a ragweed plant. They heard the train again as Mrs. Spawn threw the window open.

Liz held her breath. The sneeze grew. It filled her whole head.

"What a lovely morning," Mrs. Spawn said to the sky.

Liz held her hands over her face. She was sure she was going to burst. She heard Mrs. Spawn walk back through the office.

"Way too close for comfort," Drew whispered.

Liz sneezed. They hurried to the playground.

54

When Liz and her classmates came in for their first class, they heard Mr. Thornton's voice over the loudspeaker.

"It has been brought to my attention that someone is playing rather unpleasant tricks on our secretary, Mrs. Spawn."

The Ragged Four tried not to look at each other.

"We hope the culprit will come forward and take responsibility. The destruction of personal property is not a joke."

Allie sidled up to Liz. "This doesn't sound good."

"We didn't destroy anything," Liz said.

Mr. Thornton went on. "Whoever did these things will have to pay…"

"EEEEEKKK!"

Mr. Thornton's words were drowned in a shriek. Liz smiled.

The sixth grade had to pass the office to

get back to their homeroom. Liz heard Mrs. Spawn's voice as she, Allie, Drew, and Jinx reached the doorway.

"It was in my drawer. It frightened me to death."

"Yes!" Liz whispered.

"Hope she doesn't hurt George," Drew said quietly.

Mr. Thornton directed the class to move on. "I'm sure you have better things to do, sixth graders," he said.

"She wouldn't hurt a kitten," Liz said, as they walked on. "She isn't that horrible." She hoped she was right.

Drew looked miserable during math class, or rather, more miserable than he usually did. Drew struggled with math, even with help from Allie.

"You okay?" Liz heard Allie ask him. They were teamed up for some review.

"I wish I could see if George is all right,"Drew said.

Liz leaned over. "Relax. I have an idea."

"Not another one," Drew said. He didn't look relaxed at all.

Liz got the restroom pass and took the long route to get there. She glanced into the office. What she saw stopped her short.

Mrs. Spawn was down on the rug. She dangled a small ball of scrap paper attached to an elastic band in front of George. The kitten batted and leaped at it. Mrs. Spawn giggled.

Liz was furious. The woman was having FUN.

Mrs. Spawn looked up at Liz. "Can I help you?"

"No. I mean, no thanks," Liz said quickly. "Cute kitten."

Mrs. Spawn smiled.

At soccer practice, Liz slumped on the bench between Jinx and Drew. "What's the matter with you? Cat got your tongue?" Jinx teased. He nudged her. "Cat...get it?"

"She was playing with George," Liz said. "These pranks are way too soft. We're supposed to be getting back at her."

"She said it scared her when she opened the drawer," Drew said. "Isn't that enough?"

"Not even close," Liz said.

"She asked me to take it to our shelter after practice," Drew said. "I had to pretend that I never saw George before in my life."

"Good work," Jinx said.

But Drew didn't look comfortable. Liz knew he hated to lie.

"Yo, Drewster," Walter called. He sat down next to Drew. "How are things at the Ellis Zoo? Any escapes lately?" he asked, elbowing Drew.

Drew didn't look at him.

"What makes you ask that?" Jinx asked.

"One black cat. Who knows what else," Walter laughed. "Has Sergeant Spawn checked any of her other drawers?"

"Speaking of checking," Jinx said under his breath, "here comes Mrs. Spawn to check on us."

They all watched her approach the field. "Liz French, telephone," she shouted across to them. Then she turned back toward the building.

Liz's stomach flipped. Who would be

calling her? Maybe Drew and Jinx were right to be worried. Maybe Mrs. Spawn suspected her. Was Mrs. Spawn trying to get her inside so she could...what?

In the office Mrs. Spawn had arranged the blanket scrap on top of the papers in her IN box. George had arranged himself on the blanket. Mrs. Spawn handed the phone to Liz. She didn't even pretend not to listen.

"Hello?" Liz said.

"Liz," her mother said. "There's a GOAT eating our asters. Every single one of them. Get back here as soon as practice is over. Bring Drew. It has a bandaged leg. It must be from the shelter. I tried calling there. No one's home."

"Okay," Liz said. "Don't worry."

Mrs. Spawn stood in front of the doorway. "Was that your mother or was it your sister calling from your father's place?"

"I have to hurry back to practice," Liz said, pretending she didn't hear the question. She dodged past Mrs. Spawn and hurried outside.

6

GREAT ESCAPE

After practice Liz and Drew hurried to the office to pick up George. Then they biked to Rocky Point as fast as they could. When they got there, Jinx turned into the driveway behind them.

"Didn't want to miss any action," he said.

Liz's mother was shouting and waving her arms at a large billy goat. He munched on a clump of spinach in the vegetable garden.

Liz saw Drew flinch. "Hey, it sure beats having her yell at Pop!" she said.

Jean French saw Liz and yelled, "GET THIS THING OUT OF HERE!"

Liz, Drew, and Jinx hauled, pulled, and shoved the goat out of the garden. Liz ran for a rope, which Drew fastened around the goat's neck. The goat nibbled his shirt. George meowed in his backpack.

"Sorry, Mrs. French," he said. "This is Hector. He had an infected cut."

"I don't really care what his name is or what his problem is," Liz's mother said. She pulled up a half-chewed head of lettuce. "I'm sure he'll heal faster with all the vitamins he added to his diet today."

Jinx walked two bikes, Liz one. Drew walked Hector. Or rather, he dragged him.

"I don't understand," Drew said. "Goats are clever. But Mom has a fence rigged that

NO goat can figure out."

"Hector was in his pen this morning," Liz said. "I remember seeing him chewing the fence. Maybe he chewed through it."

"He still couldn't get out," Drew said. "There's thick wire around the outside of the pen."

As they walked the goat back to Drew's house, several passing cars honked at them. It wasn't every day people saw a goat walking along Front Street. The goat bleated loudly at each car. The third time, Liz noticed he had a scrap of green cloth stuck between his teeth.

65

"This goat needs to floss," she said. "It looks like he ate someone's shirt. Maybe he would be useful for a prank."

Drew shook his head. "Listen, Liz, I think we better not pull any more pranks. The principal's going to figure out who did the others."

"How can he?" Liz asked. "Jinx disguised his voice. You should have heard him, Drew. He sounded like he had inhaled helium. And Mrs. Spawn has no idea who put George in her drawer. You know that. And we didn't even do the coffee prank."

"What's to keep them from blaming us whether we did it or not?" Drew asked. "If they find out we did the others, you know they'll assume we did them all."

"Drew has a point, Liz," Jinx said.

Eventually they turned into the Ellis driveway.

They stopped.

"Mom's going to kill me," Drew said.

"Why?" Jinx asked.

Liz saw the reason and ran ahead. Every single gate to every single outdoor run was open. Not one animal was in sight.

Drew and Jinx secured Hector in his pen. Liz returned George to the kitten corner. She hurried back outside.

"How many animals are missing, Drew?"she asked, catching her breath.

Drew closed his eyes. "A pony, two sheep, Joe Crocksford's prize rooster, a pig, and...oh, no," he moaned.

"What?" Liz and Jinx asked in unison.

"An ostrich."

Jinx started to laugh but stopped quickly. "Sorry, Drew."

Drew looked totally desperate. "Otis— that's his name—has a heart problem. He isn't supposed to run. Mom was trying some medications on him. He'll die."

"Who would do this?" Jinx asked.

"No time to think about it. We have to find the animals," Drew said.

"You guys start," Liz said. "Go back up Front Street toward Rocky Point. I'll call Allie and Lauren. Lauren is bound to have Owen in tow. They might help. Allie and I will go around the east side of the island. Lauren can check the middle of town. Her house is right behind the library."

Allie promised to come to the shelter as quickly as possible. Liz told her to bring her camera. Then Liz called the McBride house. Lauren's mother answered.

"Oh, she's out looking for lost animals," Mrs. McBride said.

"She IS?"

"Yes. She and Owen went out about half an hour ago. I can tell her you called."

"Sure. Thank you," Liz managed.

They already knew the animals were out. How?

She ran outside. Allie skidded to a stop in front of her. "Who did this?" she asked.

"We don't have time to figure that out now. We have to get started," Liz said.

As they pedaled out Spruce Road, Allie asked, "Why did you want me to bring my camera?"

"In case we see anything suspicious," Liz shouted. "You can photograph evidence."

"Good point," Allie said. "Who do you think let the animals out? Was it an accident?"

"No way. Those gates were closed this morning," Liz said.

They biked on.

Liz thought of something. "I think I know who did this."

"Who?"

"It has to be Walter Pescatelli. Why else would he ask Drew about the 'Ellis Zoo?' He doesn't even own a pet."

"When did he say that?" Allie asked.

"Today at soccer practice," Liz replied.

"He'll do anything for a laugh," Allie said.

"Some laugh," Liz said.

They found one of the sheep caught with its head stuck through a fence near Cross Street.

"You start back with this one," Liz said. "I'll bike up as far as The Cut and then come back to help you."

"I wish I had brought rope," Allie said.

Liz pedaled away. She knew Allie would figure out a way to hold onto that sheep.

The only animal she saw was a squirrel. She biked back to Allie.

"How did you—?" Liz began. Then she

spotted the bright red of Allie's camera strap
around the sheep's neck.

Allie was holding the camera, leading the
sheep.

Liz walked beside her, pushing her bike.

"Allie, the Pescatellis live near Drew's house. How about stopping there? We can pretend we're looking for other animals."

"Great idea," Allie said. "If we see Walter, we can ask him a question or two."

They made their way down the winding Pescatelli driveway.

"What's up ahead?" Liz asked.

They could see two round figures walking in the shadows of the woods beside the driveway.

"Looks like Walter," Allie said. "And something else that looks a whole lot like a sheep."

"Your camera. Quick. I'll hold this sheep." Liz leaned her bike on a tree. Then she grabbed the strap and held on as Allie lifted her camera.

The sheep bolted. Liz stumbled against Allie just as the shutter clicked.

The sheep pulled Liz all the way to where Walter stood watching. She felt a sharp pang in her side as her right arm was nearly pulled out of its socket. Walter just stood there, laughing at her.

He was also holding a rope that was attached to the other missing sheep.

Liz's sheep baaa-ed a greeting. The other sheep nuzzled it. Allie caught up with them.

"I found this sheep in my old playhouse," Walter said, still chuckling. "Figured it belonged on the Ellis animal farm."

Liz stared at him. "Then why are you heading back to your house with it?"

"Sheep likes it here, I guess. I was just trying to turn it around for the tenth time," Walter said. "Now that you're here with its friend, it can follow you back to Drew's." He passed the rope to Allie.

As Liz and Allie walked the two sheep

back up the driveway, Allie asked, "Do you believe him?"

"No way," Liz said. "He's just covering up. He did it."

When they finally reached Drew's driveway, the shadows were lengthening, and the autumn air was turning colder. Drew and Jinx appeared from behind the house.

"We found the rooster and the pony. The pig was in the Bradleys' compost pile. She's the last, except for—"

"The ostrich?" Liz guessed, still clutching the sheep with one hand and rubbing her side with the other.

Drew nodded.

7

Otis Joins the Choir

"When does your mom get back, Drew?" Liz asked.

"She's already been here," he said. "She's driving around the island."

"And she is very, very angry," Jinx added.

"I'm supposed to meet her at Mel's. She doesn't feel like cooking supper," Drew said.

They put the two sheep back in their pen.

"We'll walk you to the diner, Drew," Jinx offered. "We can all bike home from there."

Allie slung her camera over her shoulder. "I'll meet you. I need to get my bike. I left it where we found the first sheep."

"And I left mine in the Pescatellis' driveway," Liz said. She jogged back to retrieve her bike and rode until she met up with Drew and Jinx on Spruce Road.

Jinx wobbled along, trying to ride his bike at walking pace. Drew dribbled a pebble like a soccer ball until he lost it under a wild rosebush. Liz climbed off her bike and pushed it.

"So, what's the vote now?" Jinx asked. "Did Mr. Spawn do the salt trick? Did Walter let the animals out? Or did Walter do both?"

"This is sounding way too much like a math problem," Drew muttered.

Liz realized that Jinx was staring at her.

"Liz," he began, "you had salt too. We know you're madder at Mrs. Spawn than the rest of us put together. It's okay if you..."

"IF I WHAT?" Liz said, stopping so suddenly, that Drew bumped into her.

"Forget it, Jinx," Drew said.

"No, wait," Liz said. "I want to hear the rest of it."

"I just wondered if maybe you—" Jinx began.

"DID THOSE OTHER PRANKS? NO WAY. ABSOLUTELY NOT!" Liz shouted.

"Easy, Liz." Drew patted her shoulder. "Jinx doesn't mean it. Do you, Jinx?"

"No way. Forget I said it, Liz," he said quickly.

Allie caught up with them. "I never realized how stupid sheep are," she said. "That one stuck his head through the fence to get the only clover plant on the other side. There was already tons of clover on his side."

"There are all kinds of stupid," Liz said angrily.

Drew winced. Jinx stared at his bike. Allie looked surprised, but she didn't say anything.

When they reached the diner, they sat together in a booth in the corner. No one spoke. Drew's father brought them each a soda.

"Thanks, Mr. Ellis," Jinx said.

"You all look like you've been dragged through the garden," he said. He laughed.

"'Drag it through the garden' means adding lettuce and tomato to a sandwich," Drew explained. "Dad's trying to crack a joke in diner language."

Jinx managed a chuckle.

A customer waved. "Regular or unleaded, Harry?" Jim said as he turned away to serve coffee.

"What am I going to do?" Drew finally said.

"It isn't your fault," Liz began. "I just know Walter did it."

The diner door opened. Owen charged in with Daniel. They tripped each other and landed in a heap beside the table. Lauren followed, not a hair out of place. Her wide mouth was set in a brilliant smile.

"Guess what?" Owen said from the floor.

"We found it!" Daniel chimed in.

"In the church!" Owen said.

"Found what?" Liz asked.

"THE OSTRICH!" Owen said.

"Mrs. Crocksford was airing it out," Daniel explained.

"The ostrich?" Jinx asked.

"No, the CHURCH!" Owen said.

"She had the door open," Daniel said.

"We got there just as she saw the ostrich," Lauren said.

"Is it—?" Drew began.

"Alive?" Liz finished.

"Very," Lauren said. "In the choir loft. We called your house, Drew. Your mom came to get it. She said to tell you she'll be over in a while."

"Thank you SO much," Drew said, breathing a huge sigh of relief.

"It was the least we could do. Wasn't it, Owen?" Lauren said.

Owen nodded and shoved his glasses back up on his nose. He and Daniel finally untangled themselves.

Liz remembered something. "How did you guys know the animals were missing?"

"We saw the pony wandering over to the ice-cream shop," Lauren said. "We couldn't catch it."

"Then we saw the pig at the library," Owen said.

"We did?" Daniel asked.

"YES!" Owen shouted.

"That's funny," Liz said. "Drew and Jinx found him at the Bradleys' house eating compost."

"Maybe he wanted to borrow a book before he got there," Owen said.

Daniel laughed.

Lauren didn't. She said, "We'd better be getting back." She led the two boys out of the diner.

After they left, Liz took a long drink of her soda. "How are we going to get back at Walter Pescatelli?"

"More pranks?" Allie said. "I don't know if I'm up for that."

"I don't know about Walter," Jinx said. "Are we sure he did it? He was at school all day. And he was at practice. Although having him in the net doesn't really make much difference."

"He could have come over this morning right after Drew and I left with George," Liz said.

"Hey, wait a minute," Allie said suddenly. "He was complaining to me this morning about how he had to get up so early. He had to come in at seven for extra work with Mr. Blake."

There was a pause.

Drew looked at Liz. He spoke slowly. "Liz, you closed up the kittens?"

"Of course I did," Liz said.

"Then you caught up with me part way to school," he said.

Jinx and Allie stared at her.

"Hey," Jinx said. "It's okay if you did it, Liz. All the animals are safe."

Liz couldn't breathe. Her side began to ache all over again.

Allie joined in. "Look. We know how you feel about the Sergeant Major. Drew says you wanted to use a rat instead of a cat. I mean, hey, if you wanted to use a goat, it's no problem."

Liz couldn't speak. But not for long. "WHY WOULD I WANT TO USE A GOAT? And even if I did want to use a goat—for I don't know what—there would be NO POINT in letting all those other animals out!"

Drew started making a pile of sugar packets. "You have to open all the runs to get to where the ostrich was."

"So what?" Liz asked.

"The ostrich belongs to the Spawns," Drew said very softly as his sugar pile collapsed.

8

HOLDING THE BAG

Liz could hardly pull herself out of bed. She had set the alarm even earlier for this morning. She had been dreaming about Otis. He was at the '60s dance with a neon green sign painted on his feathers: LIZ DIDN'T LET ME OUT. He danced a pretty good version of the funky chicken.

"Did you comb your hair, Liz?" her mother asked in the kitchen.

Liz ran her hand over her hair. "Can't

you even tell? I brushed it. Marla's the one who combs it," Liz said. Her voice sounded as grumpy as she felt.

"Pretty grouchy this morning," Ma said.

Liz glared at her mother. "Who do you think I get that from, you or Pop?"

Ma sighed."Early start again?" she asked.

"I'm meeting Allie. She's going to help me with my science."

This was true. In addition to Allie's prank, they were working together on the sound unit for Mr. Blake's class. Only Liz wasn't sure that Allie would want to work on the prank this morning.

The Davies house looked and sounded like a three-ring circus, as usual. Allie was standing at the sink. "Help me with the dishes?" she asked.

"Sure," Liz said. She pushed up the sleeves of her cotton shirt. She almost stepped on Tomas, who was rolling a truck around the floor.

"Beep, beep, beeeep!" he shouted.

Sasha was tossing cereal at him while Daniel let Ramon win at arm wrestling at the table. Mrs. Davies was slapping together peanut butter and honey sandwiches.

When they finished the dishes, Allie grabbed her backpack. She went straight to the shed to get her bike.

"Tools?" Liz asked.

Allie hesitated. "I don't know about this prank thing," she said.

"We vowed to see it through," Liz reminded her. "Look, Allie. You have to believe me. I haven't done anything outside of our plan. I promise."

Allie looked at her. "Okay. I believe you. But the principal's still got everyone trying to figure out who did the pranks, Liz. We should confess what we did and get it over with."

"And get blamed for the ones we didn't do? No way!" Liz said. "Thanks to you guys, our pranks are fun. There's no harm in doing the rest of them. I brought my stuff too. You do yours this morning. I'll do mine in the afternoon. Then we'll be done."

"Mine is awfully good," Allie admitted. "And it can't possibly hurt anything." A smile slowly spread across her face. "I guess it's too good to waste. I'll grab the pliers and wire."

As planned, they got to school well before Mrs. Spawn. Yesterday's timing had been much too close.

Allie went right to work on Mrs. Spawn's swivel chair. "Test it," she said through the pliers, which she was holding between her teeth.

Liz sat in the chair. She smoothed her curly hair back and held it so she would look more like Mrs. Spawn. Then she tried to spin. Nothing happened. She laughed until her stomach hurt too much.

"Let's get out of here," Allie said. "I don't want to have to climb out Mr. Thornton's window."

They worked on the science project until school began. They lined up, by pairs, the soda bottles Mr. Blake had collected. They marked each pair with one of their classmate's names. And they watched the parking lot.

"She's here!" Allie said.

"Grab the library books so it looks like we're doing something," Liz said.

They headed for the office.

"Slow down. Let her get her coat off," Liz said.

At that moment Owen and Daniel rounded the corner. "We're getting the attendance sheets," Owen said.

Their timing was perfect.

Mrs. Spawn heard Owen's voice and spun toward him. Only she didn't spin, she snapped to a stop. Allie and Liz walked faster. And faster. Until they were running. They didn't stop until they reached the library and a corner where they could laugh.

On the way back they saw Mrs. Spawn on her hands and knees peering up under her chair. Owen and Daniel hurried out of the office with the attendance sheets and huge grins.

The rest of the morning was uneventful except for science class. Mr. Blake asked Liz and Jinx to fill the soda bottles to different levels. They each made a trip to the sink with Mr. Blake's pink plastic bucket.

When all the bottles were filled, the class came to attention. Mr. Blake directed the bottle band in a rousing, out-of-tune rendition of the school song.

He smiled at them. "By graduation, we ought to have it."

"That's not until June," Jinx moaned, spilling water down his shirt.

In the restroom after lunch, Liz checked the contents of her paper bag: Marla's blue eye shadow, blusher, a jar of face cream, and a comb. She had added a tube of toothpaste, a bottle of mouthwash, and a new toothbrush from the supply of extras her mother kept for forgetful guests.

She read her typed poem one more time:

ROSES ARE RED.

VIOLETS ARE BLUE.

A MAKEOVER'S JUST

THE RIGHT THING FOR YOU.

YOUR BREATH WILL NOT STINK.
YOUR TEETH WILL BE WHITE.
THE FACE CREAM WILL MAKE YOU
LESS OF A FRIGHT.

She stuffed the bag into her backpack. The rest of the sixth grade was outside for after-lunch recess. Liz walked by the cafeteria to make sure that Mrs. Spawn and Mr. Thornton were still eating.

She walked quietly on to the office and placed the bag in the center of Mrs. Spawn's desk. She paused to picture the woman's face when she discovered the contents.

She paused too long.

"AHA! Caught holding the bag!" Mrs. Spawn rushed toward her.

Liz froze and stared.

Why hadn't she heard the click of heels in the hall? She looked at Mrs. Spawn's feet. Sneakers.

Mrs. Spawn read Liz's mind. "The better to sneak up on you, my dear."

Mrs. Spawn looked through the bag. She read the note. She frowned. She looked like a thunderstorm about to break loose. Liz's stomach tightened into a knot. She had to lean forward to ease it.

"You may stand right where you are until Mr. Thornton finishes his lunch. We will need to call your mother at Rocky Point and your father in Bellport." Mrs. Spawn spat each word out as if it could strike Liz dead.

Liz stood there for half an hour until the principal arrived. Then she stood in his office while he asked her about the pranks.

"I didn't do all of them," she said.

"What exactly do you mean?" Mr. Thornton asked.

What did she mean? Liz didn't want to get Jinx, Drew, and Allie in trouble. If she denied any of the pranks, Mr. Thornton was sure to suspect them. She couldn't very well accuse someone else of the pranks they hadn't pulled when she had no proof.

She remained silent.

Mr. Thornton suspended her for the rest of the week. He informed her that she would not be able to participate in the regional cross-country meet. Liz realized she had lost the race before she even had a chance to run. Her eyes filled with tears.

Her mother arrived.

"Liz, what's the matter?" she asked.

Liz didn't get a chance to answer.

"Your daughter is in a great deal of trouble, Mrs. French," Mr. Thornton said. He waited until Liz's father arrived. Then he told them about the pranks.

"Oh, Liz—" her mother began.

"Oh, Liz nothing," her father interrupted. "I expect better from you, Liz."

"Not now, Lou," Jean French said angrily.

Liz felt the knot in her stomach tighten. She wondered if her parents' fighting literally upset her stomach. Then she saw that the door to the office was ajar. She knew that Mrs. Spawn could hear every word her parents said.

"Liz will receive a one-week suspension," Mr. Thornton said.

"She'll come to Bellport," Pop said.

"That's ridiculous, Lou. She should be near the school so she can check in with her teachers," Ma countered.

Liz wondered if anyone would miss her if she crawled under Mr. Thornton's desk and died quietly.

9

WATER, WATER EVERYWHERE

Liz spent the rest of the school day at Rocky Point. After school she biked back to pick up the rest of her assignments for the suspension. Allie met her near the office.

She spoke softly. "Thanks for protecting us, Liz. But I don't think—

"The whole thing was my idea," Liz interrupted. "Why should all four of us get in trouble? I don't see the point."

Allie didn't look happy.

They stopped in front of Mrs. Spawn's desk.

"Just a moment. I'm getting my assistant a tissue for his glasses." Mrs. Spawn turned to the tall cabinet behind her desk. She must have repaired her chair. It swiveled smoothly.

Owen sat at Mrs. Spawn's computer table near the desk, holding a duct-taped pair of glasses with blue plastic frames. Liz wondered where his wire-rimmed glasses were.

"Looks like Mrs. Spawn has another McBride favorite," she whispered.

Allie nodded just as the tidal wave broke.

"Aaaaaaah! Eeeeeeeek!" Mrs. Spawn squawked. She looked as though she had been swimming. Water streamed, dripped, and trickled over every part of her body.

Owen was soaked, too.

But that wasn't the worst part.

"THE COMPUTER!" Mrs. Spawn shrieked.

Owen reached forward. He picked up the keyboard and flipped it over. Water drained out of it. He said, "My dad spilled coffee on ours. He said it helps if you get the wet stuff out fast."

For a moment no one spoke. The only sound was the slowing drip...drip of water everywhere.

"It will cost a fortune to replace that

99

machine," Mrs. Spawn finally said. "A fortune this school doesn't have. How did this happen? It didn't rain today. Perhaps a pipe burst." She walked around the room staring at the ceiling.

"WHAT IS THAT BUCKET DOING UP THERE?" she shouted. She pointed at the top of her cabinet. Then she remembered that Liz was in the office too. She turned on her.

"Liz French, haven't you already done enough?"

"Yikes, Liz," Allie muttered.

"I didn't—" Liz began.

"This may well be a police matter," Mrs. Spawn said.

"We'll get towels," Allie said quickly. She dragged Liz away.

They left Owen and Mrs. Spawn staring at the pink bucket that was wired to the cabinet. The bucket had red letters on the side that said *MR. BLAKE—SCIENCE. PLEASE RETURN.*

"Allie, did you see the bucket? It was Mr. Blake's," Liz said.

"So what? He would never do anything like that," Allie said as they hurried down the hall to the janitor's closet.

Liz helped her pile up towels. "He does love a good joke," she said. "Like putting a soccer shirt on Chief."

"He loves computers. He wouldn't do that," Allie repeated.

"We have been working with water," Liz said.

Allie stopped and turned to her. "Liz, anyone could have taken that bucket!"

Liz nodded. "Okay, okay. I just want to know who's doing this other stuff. I don't want to get blamed for things I didn't do. It's bad enough being in trouble for what I did.

Allie, it's like someone knows our plans."

"No one knows our plans," Allie said, "except us."

Liz didn't dare look at her. She didn't want to know that Allie didn't trust her.

They hurried back to help mop up. Walter Pescatelli had joined the rescue effort. Liz gave him a long look.

Mrs. Spawn's voice interrupted it. "You realize you will have to pay for a new computer, Liz. I tried to start it up and nothing happened. You destroyed every shred of my work."

"How can you accuse me without any proof?" Liz asked.

"You didn't back up your work on disks?" Owen asked.

Mrs. Spawn paused in her mopping and patted his head. She ignored Liz's question. "Oh, you are a sweet boy. You feel sorry for me. If only all the students were like you."

"I'll bet you say that to all the McBrides," Liz muttered under her breath.

"What happened?" Lauren asked from the doorway.

"Disaster," Mrs. Spawn said. "Thanks to Ms. French here. It's too bad Mr. Thornton had to go to a meeting on the mainland. I will have to call him away."

"Lauren, you don't think I did this, do you?" Liz asked.

Lauren wouldn't look at Liz. Liz figured she was just too good to have anything to do with someone as evil as she was. Lauren grabbed a towel to help. She stared at the computer.

"I thought you kept your computer on the other side of your desk, Mrs. Spawn," she said.

"I moved it this afternoon so your

thoughtful brother could help me with the parent mailing," Mrs. Spawn said. "This is serious vandalism." She glared at Liz.

"But I didn't do it," Liz protested.

Mrs. Spawn turned her back on Liz.

"Maybe she didn't mean for that water to go on the computer," Owen said.

"That hardly matters, dear boy," Mrs. Spawn said. "The damage is done."

Allie and Liz left the office as soon as they could. But they didn't leave before Mrs. Spawn told Liz to report to Mr. Thornton's office in the morning, with her parents— again. And maybe this time the police would join them.

They hurried to Rocky Point. "I'm calling Jinx and Drew," Liz said. "We have to prove it was Walter. Did you see how he was smiling at me in the office like he just ate a mega-batch of cookies?"

"What do you mean?" Allie asked.

"He's been near every crime scene," Liz said. "It's him." She called Jinx at his father's repair shop. Drew was helping at the diner.

"Things are slow. I'll see if Dad will let me leave," Drew said.

"Call Walter and tell him to come too," Liz said.

"Walter?"

"Kidnap him if you have to."

"Kidnap him?!" Drew asked.

"Just joking. Tell him we're going to have a french-fry feast. He'll come." Liz remembered she had no french fries. "Make that potato chips."

All three boys arrived within half an hour. The group met in Cabin 4, one of the cabins the Frenchs rented out during the summer.

Allie sat on the couch. Drew and Jinx

each flopped down on a bed. Walter sat at the small table in front of the potato chip bag. Liz paced.

"So Walter, how are the pranks going?" she asked.

"How should I know?" Walter said between mouthfuls. "You're the expert."

The sight of Walter's stuffed face made Liz feel sick.

Drew asked the next question.

"My dad said he saw you at Mel's. How come you were there with your mom this afternoon?"

Liz stared at Drew. "The diner? What's that got to do with anything?"

"I had a dentist appointment in Bellport," Walter said. "What a deal. While you were all slaving, I got to miss the whole school day, eat a hot dog, fries, and a sundae at Mel's, and then get back after school just in time for soccer."

"What a deal," Jinx echoed.

Liz didn't say anything.

The chips ran out. So did Walter. "See you around," he called as he left.

"Liz..." Drew began.

"Look, so it wasn't Walter with the computer. But there is a copy-cat prankster out there. Someone knows about the Ragged Four. You're all good at solving mysteries. Solve this one," Liz said.

"I think we should forget we ever were the Ragged Four," Drew said. "Sorry, Liz. I just think it would be better if we forgot the whole thing."

"Listen, Liz," Allie said. "You have good reason to hate Mrs. Spawn. You just got a little carried away."

"I thought you said you believed me," Liz said.

Allie hurried on. "Jinx and Drew and I talked it over. We'll help you get money for the computer."

"Allie, you really think I did those other pranks?" Liz asked.

Silence.

Liz turned to Jinx. He was busy cracking his knuckles.

"Thanks for covering for us, Liz," he said. "Look, you got too into it. It's okay. Nobody's blaming you. We're going to help you with the money."

"NOBODY'S BLAMING ME?"

"Liz, are you in there?" Jean French called.

Liz didn't answer. She stared at Drew.

"Drew, you have to believe me," she pleaded, her voice breaking.

Silence. Liz waited. She knew Drew liked to think before he spoke.

"You did have salt. You...there's the Otis thing..." he stammered.

"Drew!"

"I just don't know, Liz. I thought I believed you, but..."

"Liz, come out this minute!" her mother called. "You are suspended. No meetings with your friends until—"

"Coming!" Liz shouted.

She shoved her hands into her pockets. She felt the tools from the morning prank with Allie. That seemed years ago now. She pulled out the pliers and the wire. She threw them on the floor at Allie's feet. No one moved. Jinx forgot about cracking his knuckles.

Allie finally broke the silence. She was staring at the roll of wire. "This is the kind of wire that was holding up Mr. Blake's bucket."

10

Playing Dead

Liz lay awake most of that night. Her thoughts circled around and around with no solutions to break the pattern. Her stomach seemed to spin with them, leaving her feeling seasick in the morning.

Her mother drove her to school with her bike in the back of the car. "I want you to ride straight home after this meeting," Jean French said. Her face was set the way it looked when she fought with Pop.

"Ma, you have to believe me," Liz said. "I didn't do this prank."

"Liz, I wish I could believe you. But the evidence is too strong," Ma said. "I have to stop and pick up a few things on the way back. But you are to get straight to your chores and homework."

Mr. Thornton talked to Liz's mother and father as if Liz weren't even there. Liz clenched her fists.

"We have decided not to press charges this time," he said. "Your daughter will, however, be responsible for the cost of a new computer."

Liz felt as if she were about to explode. Tears stung her eyes. For several long moments she forgot to breathe.

Jean French shook her head. "I don't know how soon she'll be able to save up enough."

"She'll just have to deal with it," Pop interrupted.

"Don't fight," Liz begged silently.

"We'll go ahead and purchase a replacement. This will give your daughter time to earn the money."

"Thank you," Ma said.

Thank you? Liz wondered what there was to be thankful for except perhaps that the meeting was too short for her parents to have much time to argue.

"Remember, you're to bike straight home as soon as you get the rest of your books. NO detours," Ma said. "I'll be home by ten."

Liz's classmates were outside for recess. She pulled books out of her desk and shoved them into her backpack. She reached in once more to make sure she had everything. She grabbed a pen.

"Yuck," she said. Ink from the chewed

end coated her fingers. She took it over to the sink to rinse it off. She managed to drop it into the gap between the sink and a cabinet.

"What else can go wrong?" she mumbled. She stepped into the gap to reach for the pen. Crunch.

She looked down.

"Oh, no, that's what!" she said.

She recognized the small gold frames. Owen's glasses. Crushed under her sneaker. She forgot about the pen. She picked up the glasses. The frames were broken. One lens was cracked.

She slipped the glasses into her pocket. She'd have to replace them. But what was another hundred dollars when she probably owed the school thousands?

Liz biked slowly home, wishing she could forget that she was being blamed for things she didn't do. Worst of all, she wished she could forget that no one believed her, not even her best friends.

She found the list of jobs her mother had lined up for the suspension: do schoolwork, vacuum, iron, dust, bake muffins. She pulled out her favorite blueberry muffin recipe. She started to gather the ingredients. As she stooped to get a bowl out of the cupboard, something jabbed her leg.

"Ouch. What's this?" She reached into her pocket. She pulled out Owen's glasses.

Owen?

Suddenly Liz's mind began to race, and

so did Liz. She ran upstairs to her room. She had a stitch in her side by the time she got to the top of the stairs. She figured she must be getting way out of shape. But now that she couldn't run in the meet, what difference did it make? She closed the door and sat on her bed.

"I need to think slowly, carefully, the way Drew does," she said to herself.

She thought as carefully as she could. But it was hard to do it slowly.

She decided to make a list of what she needed, the way Allie would. She pulled out a pad of paper and a pen. She began a list. It was like a recipe for muffins, only this was a recipe for one last prank.

She knew she would have to be a good imitator, like Jinx. For a lonely moment she thought of how much she missed her friends. If only they could be here to help her with the things they did best. But she knew she had no choice. She'd have to solve this mystery on her own.

Almost every piece of the puzzle had fallen into place. Now all Liz needed was proof.

She wrote her list:

SALT

ANIMAL

WIRE

WATER

SIGN

PHONE CALL

TOOTHPASTE

When she finished, she began to gather what she needed in her room. She didn't want her mother to notice anything, so she hid everything except Bones under the bed. She spent the rest of the day checking off other jobs on her mother's list.

"Just you wait, Ma," Liz said to no one as she vacuumed under the refrigerator. "Just you wait, Pop. Just you wait, everyone."

Bones, who was sleeping on a stack of magazines, opened one eye to look at her and then closed it again.

That evening when she knew her mother was watching her favorite television show, Liz made the call.

"Hi, Owen? This is Liz. Hey, when I was at school today I stepped on your glasses."

"You found them?" Owen asked.

"I broke them," Liz said. "I'm sorry. Maybe they can be fixed. I'll pay for it. But you'll have to come over tomorrow and get them. I'm grounded."

"Lauren said you're in big trouble," Owen said. His voice sounded small.

"Big isn't the word. More like gigantic," Liz said.

"I'll come after school," Owen said.

Liz hoped her mother's schedule for the next day wouldn't change. She was planning a grocery run to Bellport in the afternoon and wouldn't return until after five.

* * * *

Liz woke up in the morning with a pain in her belly. She was nervous. What if Owen slipped through the trap she was setting for him?

She finished her schoolwork for the day. She thought about lunch, but she didn't feel hungry. Instead her stomach felt full of ache. She rubbed it. Some butterflies these were.

Her mother left for Bellport as planned. It was time to set the scene for her final prank.

She lined up a pepper shaker, toothpaste, a small roll of wire, and a bowl of water on the floor. She found her markers and made a big sign that read NOT GUILTY. She searched until she found Bones sleeping in the laundry basket. She carried the basket and cat into her room and set them by the bucket. Bones didn't budge.

Liz wondered if she would feel better when she lay down. But she didn't. Instead she tried curling up in a ball and pressing her hands on her stomach. This was hard because she also had to hold up her "not guilty" sign.

As she lay there, Liz lost hope. The prank was supposed to prove her innocence, but it was dumb. A pepper shaker was supposed to be salt, which she couldn't find. She had no idea where her mother had put it. The wire was the wrong kind. One tube of toothpaste was meant to be the whole bag of stuff she'd left for Mrs. Spawn. A bowl of water was supposed to be a full bucket. A cat in a basket represented all of the animals in the Ragged Island Animal Shelter. Did she look dead enough to shock the guilty party into confessing? Jinx would have played dead better. But even if she did look dead, who was going to be able to figure out that this prank combined all the other pranks and went one step further?

She heard knocking and calling. Then a door opened.

"Liz?" It wasn't Owen.

Liz tried to sit up. She needed to hide the props so whoever it was wouldn't see them. Pain stabbed her so hard she flopped back down, groaning. She couldn't move. She squeezed her eyes shut tight. Maybe she really would die.

The door suddenly flew open, knocking over the bowl of water, which splashed Bones, who hissed, spat, and scrambled under the bed.

"Liz, what's the matter?" It was Lauren's voice.

"She's DEAD!" Owen was here after all.

"She's not dead. She's just playing dead," Lauren said.

There was a short pause.

"Okay, she's not dead," Owen said. "But she's not playing, either."

Liz opened her eyes. At first all she could see was Owen's pale moon face. Lauren was kneeling beside him. Her hair was messy. One shirttail was out. Amazing. Her eyes looked red and wet. She looked like she was spinning slowly.

Liz tried to speak. All that came out was a whimper. "I knew Owen wasn't tall enough to wire the bucket..."

"We're Ragged Fours too," he said, proudly putting an arm on his sister's shoulder.

"That makes six," Liz moaned.

He stared at her very closely. Suddenly he turned and ran.

Liz could hear him talking on the telephone, giving her address. He was probably calling the police to turn her in. She could just picture him standing there with his owl eyes and his green shirt with a large, ragged hole.

11

RETURN FROM THE DEAD

Liz dreamed that she was dead. No one missed her. Her parents were too busy fighting to notice that she was gone. She had lost all of her...

"She's waking up, Allie."

Friends?

Jinx.

"It's about time."

Allie.

She felt a gentle hand on her arm.

Liz opened her eyes.

Drew.

Liz tried to move. She felt a thick bandage around her middle.

"We thought you were never going to wake up," Allie said.

"Liz?" Ma leaned close from the other side of the bed.

"Hey, pal," Pop said. He put a cool hand on Liz's forehead. "How are you feeling?"

"Sleepy," Liz said. The stabbing pain was

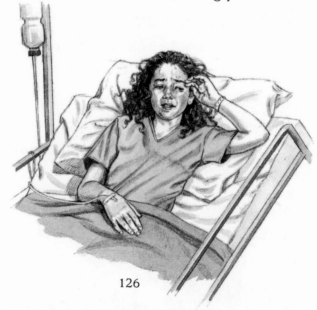

126

gone. It had been replaced by a general soreness that was much easier to live with.

"You certainly are sleepy," her mother said. "You woke up once before in the recovery room. Don't you remember?"

Liz tried to think. She had a vague image of her parents. But she thought they were part of her dream.

"Thank goodness you're all right," Ma said.

"What happened?" Liz asked. She noticed the metal bar on the side of the bed and the television mounted near the ceiling.

"You're in Bellport Hospital. Owen called the ambulance. You had emergency surgery," her father said. "They got your appendix out just before it would have burst."

"I like it when you two don't fight," Liz said.

"So do I," her mother said, glancing at her father.

"Guess that makes three of us," Pop agreed.

"Liz," Ma said. "Why didn't you tell us you weren't feeling well?"

Liz thought about that for a moment. "I didn't know it was anything bad. I guess I just thought that your fighting or everyone blaming me for stuff I didn't do made me sick to my stomach."

Pop laughed a little. "Can't say as I blame you for that. But still, you should have told us. We have to keep the communication lines open."

Allie, Drew, and Jinx slipped out of the room and shut the door quietly.

Liz stared at her parents. "Maybe I should have said something. It did seem a little weird that I suddenly had a weak stomach.

But you guys were always too busy not getting along."

Ma and Pop both looked embarrassed.

Ma said, "I know we haven't exactly been setting a superb example of communication. In fact, I think arguing just got to be a habit."

"And not a very good one," Pop agreed. "We have to give you a chance to get a word in edgewise if we're going to insist you tell us what's bothering you."

"Maybe it's more difficult living separately," Ma said. "But that doesn't mean we're no longer a family. You being so sick woke us up."

"I'm glad my appendix was good for something," Liz said, beginning to smile.

Ma and Pop laughed.

"I hope you won't ever need to take such desperate measures again," Ma said.

"If you had allowed me to take her to Bellport for the suspension, it wouldn't have been such a close call," Pop said, frowning. "She would have been close to the hospital."

"Dad!" Liz said. "You're arguing again, and I'm telling you that it bothers me!"

Her father held up his hands. "Okay, okay. That's good, clear communication, Liz."

"Peace?" Ma asked.

"Peace," Pop said.

Not for long, Liz thought. But she planned to enjoy every minute of it.

"Mind if we go grab a bite?" Pop asked.

"We'll give you some time with your other visitors," Ma added.

"No fighting over the ketchup," Liz said.

They gave her a gentle, double hug.

Allie, Drew, and Jinx hurried back into the room after Ma and Pop left.

"Have you used the bed pan yet?" Jinx asked.

"Is the food any good?" Allie asked.

"All she can eat is ice cream," Drew announced.

"I haven't eaten anything yet," Liz said. "But I solved the mystery."

No one said anything for a moment.

"I don't blame you for not believing me," Liz said. "There was no proof it was anyone else. But I broke Owen's glasses in the

131

science room. They jabbed into my leg through my pocket. That got me thinking. It was the clue that made the others click into place. I realized Owen was around for every prank. The one thing I wasn't sure about was the bucket rig. He's way too small to wire it. I couldn't believe Lauren would help. She's such a goody—"

"Goody." Lauren finished the sentence as she stepped into the room, towing her brother. Her hair and her shirttails were back in place. "We came to apologize, didn't we, Owen?" she said.

Owen shuffled his feet, making his sneakers squeak on the bright hospital floor.

"Owen heard you guys at the beach planning your pranks," Lauren began.

"Were you the crash we heard, Owen?" Jinx asked. "We thought it was our bikes falling over."

"I ran into them," Owen said, pushing his smudged glasses up on his nose. "But I picked them back up. I didn't see them."

Jinx said, "I can't imagine why." He pulled a kerchief out of his pocket. He handed it to Owen, who pulled his glasses off and tried, unsuccessfully, to clean them.

Lauren continued. "Owen told me what you were planning. I decided I was sick of being such a teacher's pet. You all look like you have so much fun. So I planned some pranks too. Owen helped me."

Owen nodded.

"He watched me salt the coffee and decided I hadn't put in quite enough."

"And his aim wasn't too good," Liz said, smiling. She looked at Jinx, Drew, and Allie. "That was the first clue."

Lauren went on. "But it really wasn't his fault. It was all my idea."

133

Owen nodded harder. His glasses slid back down his nose.

"I asked him to go to the shelter. Dr. Ellis is always telling people to stop by and see if they want to adopt a pet. I figured she wouldn't mind if we borrowed one. I told Owen to borrow a rat. I wanted to put it in Mrs. Spawn's purse."

"That's exactly what I wanted to do," Liz said.

"You did?" Lauren asked. She smiled for the first time.

"But Drew wouldn't let me," Liz said.

"A goat," Owen said.

"What?" Drew asked.

"I wanted a goat for Daniel's yard. He would laugh. I forgot all about the rat. I got the gates mixed up. Then the goat ate my shirt."

"Second clue," Liz said, pointing to the

hole in the back of Owen's shirt.

He went on. "The goat ran away. I chased it. But then the ostrich chased me. So I went on to school."

"He told me he couldn't get me a rat that day," Lauren said. "Then later he told me why. That's how we knew to go look for all the animals."

"I made up the part about the pig getting a book out of the library," Owen said, turning a light shade of pink.

Liz held up three fingers.

"Clue number three," Allie said.

"I saved the best, or maybe I should call it the worst, prank for last," Lauren went on. "I rigged the water to land on Mrs. Spawn. I didn't plan on having her move the computer. Owen volunteered to help her."

"I wanted to see what happened," Owen said.

Lauren looked a little angry and a little like she wanted to laugh. "And to see, you had to get up close each time, especially after you lost your good glasses getting that bucket for me," she said.

"Clue number four," Jinx said.

Liz nodded.

"Liz, I'm really sorry I didn't say anything when Mrs. Spawn blamed you for that. I don't know what happened to me. It was like I froze. I couldn't make myself admit it." Tears filled Lauren's eyes and then made dark mascara trails down her cheeks. Liz didn't know what to say.

"We weren't as good a prank team as you," Owen said.

"Hold on just a minute," Liz said. "Don't forget I was the only one who got caught. I wasn't very good at it at all."

"You certainly were good at your last one," Lauren said, sniffling. "Owen was sure you were dead."

"Only until I really looked," Owen said.

"I was trying to surprise you into confessing," Liz said. "It was a pretty stupid idea. It backfired."

"Maybe it backfired, but it also worked," Lauren said.

"Why did you come with Owen?" Liz asked her.

"I was afraid that you were on to him. I didn't want him to have to face you alone, when it was all my idea," Lauren said.

"I'm that scary?" Liz asked.

"When you're dead you are," Owen said.

Everyone laughed.

"I'm going to talk to Mrs. Spawn today," Lauren said. She looked very uneasy.

Liz felt sorry for her, a goody-goody gone bad. "We'll help with the computer," she said.

"We'll what?" Jinx asked.

Drew got him in a hammer lock.

"I yield!" Jinx shouted.

"Definitely," Allie said to Lauren. "We're in this together."

"I'm in it too," Owen said.

"I guess you did a little pranking yourself," Liz said.

"I did a lot," Owen replied.

12

A LAUGHING MATTER

There was a tap on the door. "May I join you?"

Liz thought she recognized the voice. But she couldn't quite believe it. "Come in," she said.

Mrs. Spawn set a large, prickly cactus on the table beside the bed. It had a purple bow just the color of her ruined suit. On a pink card the words *With Deepest Sympathy* had been crossed out. Over them Mrs.

Spawn had written *Get Well Soon*.

"Thank you," Liz said, trying her best to sound sincere. She glared at Allie, who was trying not to giggle.

Mrs. Spawn stood very straight. She looked down her nose at Liz. "I want you to know that I forgive you," she said. "I have decided to pay for the cleaning of my suit. And I plan to adopt the kitten."

"You mean George?" Drew asked.

"His name is not George. It is Smudge," Mrs. Spawn said firmly.

"Okay, okay," Drew said quickly.

She turned to Jinx. "I'll be able to use that kitty litter I won after all. And maybe my bonus too. Although I don't yet know what it is."

Jinx groaned. "You recognized my voice?"

"No. I recognized your dog's voice," Mrs. Spawn said.

"Chief?" Jinx asked. "You're kidding."

"Yes, I am," Mrs. Spawn said.

She waited. "You may laugh if you wish. It was a joke."

Everyone forced a laugh, as ordered.

"You'll be glad to know that Otis is going to be all right," she went on.

"Otis?" Jinx asked.

"Her ostrich, remember?" Drew said.

"Oh, yeah," Jinx said.

Mrs. Spawn's eyebrows lowered. She stared hard at Liz. "That leaves the computer."

"Liz didn't do all the pranks, Mrs. Spawn," Owen interrupted.

Everyone looked carefully around the room.

"I wired up the bucket," Lauren began.

"We all did pranks," Owen said.

Mrs. Spawn snapped to attention. "Whatever do you mean?"

Liz began, "We didn't all do everything. But—"

"we all did something," Lauren finished for her.

"Lauren, I must say, I am shocked and disappointed in you," Mrs. Spawn said.

"She had trouble being really bad, Mrs. Spawn," Liz said. "Didn't you notice how she was always around helping to clean things up? She helped rescue Otis too."

Mrs. Spawn looked confused. "Why me? Why did you play these pranks on me?"

For a moment no one said anything. Then one by one all eyes came to rest on Liz. She took a deep breath. She remembered what Pop had said about lines of communication.

"It was my idea," she said. "I was really mad at you."

Mrs. Spawn looked surprised. "Why on earth?"

"You kept making comments."

"Comments?" Mrs. Spawn asked.

"About my parents; about the divorce," Liz finally managed.

"I would never do such a thing," Mrs. Spawn said.

"You always made a big deal about two addresses and stuff like that," Liz said.

"I just like to keep track, in case of emergencies," Mrs. Spawn said. She looked angry and something else. Sorry?

"We all had reasons," Allie said.

Mrs. Spawn looked even more astonished. "You ALL had reasons?"

"They aren't big-deal reasons," Jinx said quickly, glancing at Lauren.

Liz could see he had no desire to discuss his crush on Lauren with Mrs. Spawn, particularly in front of Lauren.

"That's right," Liz said. "They were little things. The pranks were supposed to be revenge."

"But they were supposed to be funny revenge," Drew said.

"So you'd lighten up a little," Allie said. "And you have."

Mrs. Spawn seemed confused.

"You just cracked a joke about Chief," Liz reminded her.

"Oh. Yes, I did," Mrs. Spawn said. "I didn't realize I was being so unpleasant at school. I was just trying to do my job." She paused for a moment and looked at Liz. "I used the mouthwash."

Liz felt her face get hot.

"I must try to be more pleasant. But you all know that rules are rules. We have to keep up the standards at our school."

No one spoke.

Mrs. Spawn began to smile. "There I go again. Let me start over with some good news for all of you. The computer can be repaired after all. That won't cost as much as replacing it. And a specialist was able to recover most of my work. Owen's fast thinking saved the day."

"Owen's fast thinking saved me too," Liz said.

"Yay, me!" Owen said.

"Yay, YOU?" Lauren said. "If it weren't for you—" she stopped, shaking her head. Then she grabbed him and spun him around.

Owen giggled. His glasses ended up hanging from one ear. For a moment he and his sister looked like they were dancing.

"Uh-oh, I think I just figured out a way to raise some money," Liz said.

"How?" Jinx asked. "Win the lottery?"

"A dance," she said.

"A whole lot of dances!" Lauren shouted. She leaped into a cheerleader jump. When she landed she said, "Thanks, everybody." She paused, smiled, and looked straight at Jinx. "Thanks for offering to help."

Jinx turned bright red. Then a big, goofy grin spread across his face.

"Dances are fine by me," Mrs. Spawn said. She started into her slow motion twist.

"No screaming guitars," Drew said.

Suddenly Liz sneezed.

"You must be allergic to dances," Allie said.

Liz's belly ached when she laughed. But she didn't mind.

ABOUT THE AUTHOR

Rosie Bensen lives in Maine with her husband, Gary, her children, Mike and Julia, and pets who come from an animal shelter like the one at Drew's house on Ragged Island. In addition to writing stories and poetry, she teaches a combination of art and writing called Wordplay. She also loves to hike, knit, sing, grow flowers, and spend time on a Maine island in Muscongus Bay.